Finders Keepers for Franklin

First U.S. hardcover edition 1998

Text copyright © 1997 by Paulette Bourgeois
Illustrations copyright © 1997 by Brenda Clark
Interior illustrations prepared with the assistance of
Shelley Southern.

Franklin and the Franklin character are trade marks of
Kids Can Press Ltd.

Kids Can Press Ltd. acknowledges with appreciation the
assistance of the Canada Council and the Ontario Arts
Council in the production of this book.

Published in Canada by: Published in the U.S. by:
Kids Can Press Ltd.   Kids Can Press Ltd.
29 Birch Avenue   85 River Rock Drive, Suite 202
Toronto, ON M4V 1E2   Buffalo, NY 14207

Printed in Hong Kong by Wing King Tong Co. Ltd.

KCP/CM 97 0 9 8 7 6 5 4 3 2 1

Canadian Cataloguing in Publication Data

Bourgeois, Paulette
    Finders keepers for Franklin

ISBN 1-55074-368-6

I. Clark, Brenda. II. Title.

PS8553.085477F56 1997   jC813'.54   C97-930952-2
PZ7.B68Fi 1997

Finders Keepers for Franklin

Written by Paulette Bourgeois
Illustrated by Brenda Clark

Kids Can Press Ltd.

FRANKLIN could count by twos and tie his shoes. He was good at seeing things that others missed. Once Franklin found a lucky four-leaf clover. Another time, he found the keys his mother had lost. But one day Franklin found something special.

Franklin was walking to the park when he spotted a flash of blue. Something was lying by the side of the path.

"Oh!" said Franklin, picking it up. "A camera!"

He had never found anything quite so wonderful before.

Franklin looked through the viewfinder.
He imagined he was a photographer, just like
Grandma, who took last summer's pictures.

"Say 'Cheese!'" he said.

Franklin pretended to click the clicker.

Then he noticed that somebody had already
taken one picture.

As soon as Franklin got to the park, he showed the camera to his friends.

"Wow," said Moose. "Is that yours?"

"Not exactly," said Franklin. "I found it."

Beaver shrugged. "Finders keepers," she said.

"Well, I looked, but there's no name on the camera," said Franklin.

"Then it's yours," insisted Beaver.

"It's not like stealing," said Moose. "You found it."

Still, Franklin knew he wasn't allowed to keep things that didn't belong to him.

He decided to find the owner later.

Just then, Beaver made a funny face.
"That's good!" said Franklin.
He snapped a picture.

"Me too! Me too!" cried Moose and Rabbit.
Before he knew it, Franklin had used the
rest of the film.

Franklin took the film out of the camera and put it in his marble bag.

"I'll have to get more film," he said.

"Are you keeping the camera?" asked Moose.

Franklin looked surprised.

"Whoops! I almost forgot that it isn't mine," said Franklin. "I'd better find out who lost it."

"Maybe the owner will be mad because you used the camera," Beaver said.

Franklin gulped. "I didn't think of that."

Now Franklin wasn't sure what to do. He didn't like it when someone was angry with him.

Franklin thought for a while.

After his friends left, he put the camera back where he'd found it.

"That's better," he sighed. "Now nobody will be mad at me."

Franklin went home and ate a nice supper.

After supper, Franklin's father wanted to play marbles. When Franklin opened his marble bag, the film rolled out.

"What's that?" asked Franklin's father.

"Ummm," said Franklin.

His father waited patiently.

Finally, Franklin blurted out the whole story — finding the camera, using it and then putting the camera back.

"So you used something that didn't belong to you?" asked his father.

"Not on purpose," answered Franklin. "It just sort of happened."

"What do you think should happen now?" said his father.

Franklin thought and thought.

"Maybe we could get the camera and try to find the owner," he said finally.

So Franklin and his father got the camera, made signs and posted them in the park.

They waited a week, but nobody claimed the camera.

Then they went to the police station and told the officers that they'd found a camera. Still nobody claimed it.

Franklin took the film to be developed. He bought a new roll of film with his allowance and popped it into the camera.

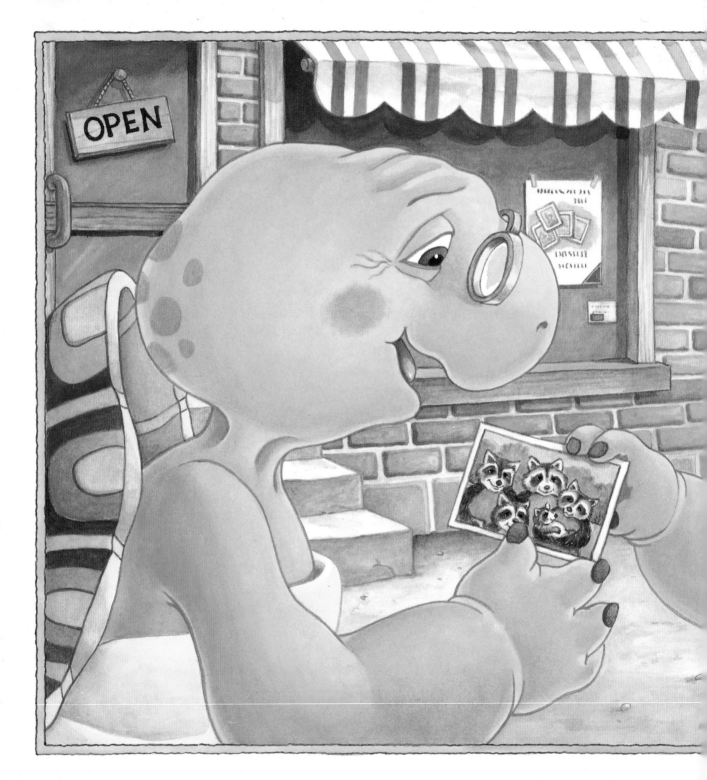

The next day, the pictures were ready.
Franklin held up a photo of Raccoon's family.
"I know who owns the camera!" he shouted.
"Raccoon must have taken a picture just before
he lost the camera. And he's been away, so he
didn't see our signs."

Franklin returned the camera to Raccoon
and apologized for using his film.

Raccoon wasn't mad at all. He was so happy
to have his camera back that he shared his
snack with Franklin.

"Cheese!" said Franklin, smiling.

And Raccoon snapped a picture.